RUPERT ROCHESTER & ELSIE POCKET

THREE STORIES

C.P.T. JENNINGS

RUPERT ROCHESTER & ELSIE POCKET
THREE STORIES

RED FEATHER PRESS NEW YORK

2018

Rupert Rochester & Elsie Pocket
Three Stories

Contents

ELSIE POCKET

Her Sad Yet Fortunate Story

In loving memory of my friend Louise
who would have liked this little adventure.

Has anyone ever told you the story of Elsie Pocket, that peculiar person who works magic in the gardens at 13 Truffle Avenue? No? Well, I will tell you then, because it's a very interesting story indeed.

Most people, if they know of Elsie at all, think she is rather odd and very homely, in spite of the pink glow that enlivens her cheeks. Now that she's grown up and no one can tell her what to wear, she's always dressed in overalls, because, of course, she's usually to be found digging in the dirt. She doesn't smile very often, but even so, that is a lot more than not at all, which was once the case.

And with good reason. That is what I'm going to tell you about.

Once upon a time, Elsie Pocket was actually Her Royal Highness, Elsina Pookatina. She was born in a far away and exotic land, the beautiful, smiling baby of the handsome Lord Oliver Pookatina and his beautiful lady, Zaha Pookatina.

They lived in what passed for a palace in that kingdom, and Elsina, her mother, and her father played with each other every day, almost all the live- long day. They loved each other dearly.

Elsie smiled all the time in those days, and got to go on camel rides whenever she wanted. It really was a perfect life for a child.

But when Elsina Pookatina was only ten, her father's beastly brother, Uncle Frederick Pookatina, staged a coup d'état, which means he took over the kingdom. He even claimed that Lord Oliver spent TOO MUCH TIME with his wife and little daughter! So he stabbed his brother and chased Elsina and her mother out of the kingdom.

Now it was possibly true that Lord Oliver had spent a little too much time with his family, in that he had been a very disorganized and unambitious ruler, so -- for a short while -- the people were happy to settle for Uncle Frederick, who was insanely organized and maniacally ambitious. It is said that he made the cockroaches march in formation!

So Elsie (it was easier to escape if she changed her name from Elsina and went incognito) and her mother fled, driven north by the army, which had been totally fooled by Uncle Frederick's false charm. For days, with nothing but the clothes on their backs, Elsie and her mother sneaked through city streets....

climbed over the high mountains surrounding the city,

and crossed the great dry desert, all the while avoiding Uncle Frederick's henchmen, who had been ordered to shoot on sight. It was a terrible journey.

But at last they reached the sea. They scrambled down the steep sea-cliff just as the soldiers appeared at the top, and they leaped into the tiny boat that was miraculously awaiting them.

For two whole weeks they tossed on the sea, with nothing to eat but the little sardines that took pity and jumped into the boat, sacrificing themselves, and nothing to drink but the canister of water they found under the seat in the boat. Starving, grieving, sunburned, weak, and in rags, they made landfall at last.

By then, tragically, Elsie's mother had given up all hope. "We're almost there, Mama!" Elsie had been saying for days in her most encouraging tone although she had no idea where they were, even when towering skyscrapers appeared on the distant horizon. But any land was better than no land, and Elsie paddled furiously. She needed to get her poor mama to some place safe and warm.

At long last, they came to a tiny little dock that seemed suitable for such a modest boat as theirs. Besides, all the bigger docks had burly bustling men, and after being chased by Uncle Frederick's soldiers, Elsie didn't trust burly, bustling men.

She paddled up to the little dock and tied their boat to it, then helped her mother to climb up out of the boat. For a long time, they just sat there, their feet dangling over the edge. "Now what?" thought Elsie. It was nice not to be in the boat anymore, but she was too tired to do anything, and her mother could scarcely sit up, let alone walk.

"You two ladies need help?" said a soft, gentle voice. It was one of the burly, bustling men, but he wasn't frightening at all.

He took Elsie and her mother to a big, shabby house, where they were given a room to themselves and three square meals a day.

The gruff woman who worked there took them to a government office where she bullied the man in charge until he gave them political asylum, which meant that they could never be sent back to Uncle Frederick. The man read off a long list of things they weren't allowed to do and then stamped some papers. Because he was a bad speller and wanted words to be easy, he changed their last name from Pookatina to Pocket.

Now, by some miracle, Elsie and her mother had come to the land where Elsie's other uncle lived. His name was Bob Pocket (the same government official had stamped Bob's papers), and he had come to live there years before, because he didn't really like the royal life. He wanted to be more modern. And he was: he had a very good job at an internet company.

But he had been sick with worry ever since hearing about the coup d'état back home. He had no idea that his little niece (Elsie had been a tiny baby when he last saw her) and his sister-in-law had just arrived in his adopted city. He thought that Uncle Frederick must have killed them (he had always been suspicious of his brother Frederick), or that they were perhaps in hiding thousands of miles away.

Elsie had never forgotten about her Uncle Bob, who had been her father's favorite brother. One day when her mother was napping, Elsie set out to find him. She went to three different internet companies before she found the right one. The security guard didn't want to let such a scraggly girl in, but when he wasn't looking, Elsie dashed past and hopped into the elevator.

She recognized her uncle instantly from the portrait of him that had hung in the dining room back in the palace. "Uncle Bob!" she said, her voice a little trembly. He turned around and, somehow, even though she was all grown up, he knew who she was and swept her up into his strong arms. Then he sat her down with cookies and milk, and she told him everything, including the sad fact that her mother hadn't long for this world.

So Bob closed his office, and they returned to the little room where Elsie lived with her mother just in time for Bob to promise that he would look after Elsie. "Make sure she gets a good education," said Elsie's mother, "so that she can take care of herself. I wish I had. I love you both, but I've had enough of this cruel, beautiful world. Goodbye." And with that, she drew her last breath.

Bob was true to his word. He moved Elsie into his own very nice apartment. He sent her to an excellent school for girls where she had every opportunity, although as it turned out, Elsie's only interest was in the gardens. After all she'd been through, Elsie had had enough of people's ways, if not of people.

She loved the peace and quiet to be found in the garden, and the uncomplicated busy-ness of the animals and birds who inhabited it, and the gardener, Henry, who felt as she did about the world. Henry taught her everything he knew.

In the meantime, Bob quit his job at the internet company and went to manage a soup kitchen, because he wanted to help people and find more meaning in his life. He was much happier there, but it meant that he made a lot less money, and one day he said to his niece, " You're old enough to earn your own living now, Elsie."

So Elsie set out to look for a job in a garden. She knocked on lots of doors at houses with gardens, but most of them were slammed in her face before she had a chance to say a word.

Not at 13 Truffle Avenue though. Just as she had begun to think no one was home, the door was opened by an old man with sharp yet kindly eyes. His name was Sir Rupert Beattie-Felford, and he lived in the house by himself. He had once been quite an important man, but now he was old and forgotten, even by his only child. She never came to visit, although she did send her son – also named Rupert, although his last name happened to be Rochester – to stay whenever she needed a babysitter.

Sir Rupert studied Elsie for about thirty seconds, then said, "You've come at exactly the right time. I'm sorely in need of a gardener."

Elsie transformed the gardens at 13 Truffle Avenue, and her quiet presence made Sir Rupert happy for the rest of his days. When the weather was nice, which it often was, he and Elsie had their tea in the garden and chatted about everything under the sun.

After old Sir Rupert died --at the end of a long and very rich life – his daughter moved into the house with her creepy husband and very shy son. Elsie stayed on, quietly making the gardens beautiful, year after year. Both parents were usually away, and the little boy Rupert lived in the house, looked after by the army of servants his mother had hired. Elsie often wondered what he was up to.

But that is for another story.

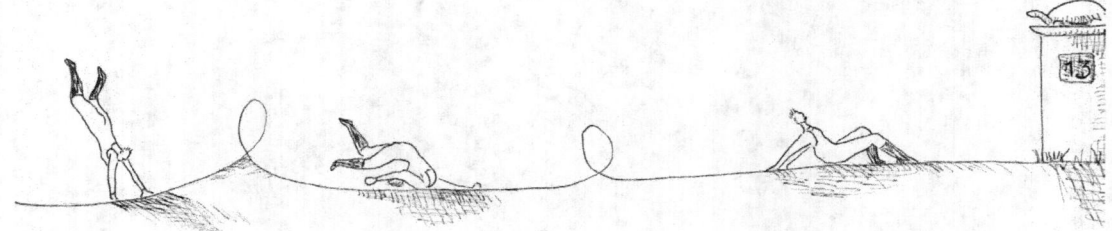

Rupert Rochester and Elsie Pocket
The story of a boy, a gardener, and a camera

For my American girls,
Rebecca, Sophie, Lucy, Elnie, and Sarah
and my English boys,
Christopher and Diego

Until the age of nine, Rupert Rochester was a very spoiled little boy. He lived in a grand house in quite a large city ~ a house that was full of toys, gadgets, antique furniture, knick-knacks, jewels, silver, house plants, and servants. Even though he hardly ever saw his parents, he wanted for nothing in the material sense. The one thing he might have liked was companionship, but since he'd never had it, he didn't really know what it was.

Rupert lived in a very large house...

To the servants, Rupert was a little like one of the house plants, and simply needed to be watered regularly. They did sometimes talk about him behind his back though. A few of them laughed at him and said things like, "what a pathetic little pipsqueak," while others felt sorry for him and said, "poor little sod." The cook sometimes even patted his head.

...where several servants took care of him.

Rupert's mother was an Important Person who was always off making speeches in foreign countries. She was a Good Person, but that didn't mean she was a particularly Nice Person – she cared very much about children as a group, but she wasn't all that fond of individual children. She never really knew what to say to her little boy Rupert.

Rupert's mother was an Important Person,

Rupert's father wasn't nearly as important as his mother, but he liked money and made lots of it, no one was quite sure how. He was neither Good nor Nice, and didn't pretend to be. In fact, he had only married Rupert's mother so that he could live in the lovely big house that had been in her family for hundreds of years, but then he got tired of that and hardly ever came home. He actively disliked all children and didn't concern himself with Rupert at all.

The servants, formal as they were, came closer to being family than Rupert's own parents.

and his father wasn't very nice.

Rupert had a lot of fancy gadgets, Christmas and birthday presents from his mother that helped her to believe she was a good parent (his father didn't bother). He liked most of them okay – his 3 computers, his GPS receiver, and his MP3 player, but the only one that he never grew tired of (and it actually wasn't all that fancy) was his camera. You could almost say that Rupert lived and breathed through his camera. He spent large chunks of each day taking pictures of everything in the house and garden, and of all the servants, from every conceivable angle.

Rupert spent a great deal of time taking pictures from funny places.

All in all, it was a very strange, storybook, old-fashioned, lonely, peculiar life to be living in this day and age - or so it would have seemed to almost anyone else. But it was the only life little Rupert had ever known, and in his own funny way he was happy.

Then, overnight, tragedy struck.

In his own funny way, Rupert was happy.

News came that his mother, while attending Important Meetings in Amman, Jordan, went to visit Kerak Castle and somehow fell off a parapet. Part of the parapet fell with her, and she was killed outright. It was a strange thing to have happened, particularly as she had always thought she would be kidnapped and held for ransom.

And then one day, tragedy struck.

The terrible news gave his father the excuse he'd been hoping for to move to Switzerland with his blond bombshell girlfriend, taking with him the money from all of his and his dead wife's bank accounts. Fortunately, he couldn't take the beautiful house that was the only home Rupert had ever known. It would have been difficult if not impossible to load it on a plane, or even a train, to Switzerland.

Rupert's father went to Switzerland with his blond bombshell
girlfriend and all the money.

One by one, the servants left. A couple of them had the grace to look guilty as they slouched out. In a way it was a relief to Rupert to see them go, because at least now he didn't have to worry about paying them. But it was also a big problem, as Rupert had no idea how to take care of himself. His only real skill was in taking pictures, and now half the fun of that was gone too, since all his best subjects had abandoned him.

One by one the servants left.

But Rupert was a positive thinker. When the last of the servants had gone, he stood in the middle of the hallway holding his camera and tried to think of new angles to shoot from. It was just as he was trying to climb up on the hallway chandelier from the banister without falling down that he noticed, out the landing window, a lone figure hunched over the bed of irises, columbine, and fairy roses.

He noticed a lone figure in the garden.

He climbed off the banister, ran downstairs to the front door, and opened it. He stood in the doorway for several minutes before finally calling out. "Hey! Pardon me!" Slowly, holding her back as though it hurt, the person stood up and turned around. Rupert recognized the dour face of Elsie Pocket, the gardener. Hadn't she heard the news? He wondered.

"Haven't you heard the news?" he shouted.

Elsie Pocket glanced down at the chunk of irises in her hand (she had been separating the bulbs) and back up at the little boy in the doorway. Slowly she shook her head.

"Haven't you heard the news?" he shouted.

Rupert was not very good at shouting (or even at talking, for that matter), so he came down the steps and ran up the garden path until he was near enough to Elsie Pocket that she could hear his whispery voice. He explained to her everything that had happened, ending with, "So there isn't any money."

Elsie Pocket's face was set in a perpetual scowl. Rupert didn't know it, but almost no one had ever seen Elsie smile. In fact, the other servants used to talk about Elsie behind her back just the way they did about Rupert, but none of them ever felt sorry for her as they sometimes had for him. Everyone assumed, because Elsie was homely, solemn, and quiet, that she must be rather nasty. Rupert didn't think this; he just thought that she might not like the idea that she wasn't going to be paid.

Elsie's face was set in a perpetual scowl.

For a minute, Elsie stared at Rupert, and Rupert stared right back. Then she nodded slowly. "I hadn't heard," she said. Her voice was grumbly like a thunderstorm, or a person who never spoke very much. She stuck her trowel in her hip pocket and, turning, walked slowly away from Rupert until she disappeared out the garden gate.

She disappeared out the garden gate.

Rupert turned around and went slowly back to the house, feeling strangely as though he would have liked Elsie Pocket to stay. But this was it. He was on his own now. He wasn't the kind of little boy that people were likely to remember and want to come find. He knew he had a lot to figure out, but he pushed it to the back of his mind. He wandered aimlessly around the house, not even lured by the prospect of taking photographs of a sensational sunset through the attic window. Finally, overwhelmed by inertia, he let himself into the linen closet, which smelled like lavender, and fell asleep.

The next thing he knew he was staring up into the dimly lit face of Elsie Pocket. She was standing over him, in a green dress (she looked a little odd without her overalls) and with a duffel bag containing her few belongings in one hand. "It smells like lavender in here," she said. "Your cocoa's getting cold."

"It smells like lavender in here," she said.

And so began Rupert and Elsie's life together. Rupert made a snap decision that Elsie's room should be the one his own mother had slept in as a child, at the top of the house just beneath the attic. He had always liked that room, which still contained dolls, a wooden hobby horse, and a very large doll house, and he hoped that Elsie would like it too.

She did!

Rupert had always liked that room.

After a few days, Rupert got used to Elsie, and Elsie to Rupert. Neither of them had much to say, which meant that they learned to communicate mostly in other ways. Neither of them smiled very much either. Elsie in fact was a real sourpuss, the lines around her mouth and above her eyes set from years of grim expressions. For Elsie had experienced tragedies of her own, as you may have already heard.

It must be said, she sometimes complained. "My goodness, there's a lot to keep clean." "I barely have time for the garden." "All these stairs!"

"So many stairs!"

"So many rooms, too many hallways." "Easy to get lost around here." But between the two of them they just about managed to keep things from falling apart. While not a world-class cook, Elsie made meals that Rupert liked. They had mashed potatoes and apple cobbler almost every night.

"So many rooms! Too many hallways!"

She let Rupert pick out his own outfits every day.

Rupert didn't really have very many outfits.

She taught him how to separate the iris bulbs and
dead-head the roses.

Rupert thought he might have a green thumb!

She sent him off to his room right after supper every night so that they might each have some time alone. All in all, things were satisfactory.

But Elsie was quickly coming to the realization that it took a LOT of money to run a big house like Rupert's, even for two such small people. They had already spent most of her savings, and she had counted the coins in Rupert's piggy bank: $17.23. She looked around at all the stuff in the house, the antique furniture, knick-knacks, jewels, and silver, thinking of what it was worth, but quickly dismissed the idea of trying to sell it on ebay. Rupert was surely traumatized enough after all the recent tragedy without having all those familiar things sold out from under him (if she had bothered to ask him, she would have learned he didn't care).

What a lot of useless stuff!

As Elsie sat at the kitchen table, her head in her hands, worrying about their money shortage, Rupert popped around a corner and snapped a picture of her. Then he ducked under the table, popped up on the other side, and snapped another. In no time flat he'd taken five or six, leaving Elsie breathless with self-consciousness. "What do you do with all those pictures, boy?" she asked in her gruff, self-conscious way.

"Nothing much," said Rupert shyly.

What you need is a good website," said Elsie. "My brother makes good websites, when he's not busy feeding the poor."

"Feeding the poor?" repeated Rupert. He wasn't all that clear on who "the poor" were. He hadn't seen much of the world. He only had a vague idea that living in a big house with lots of stuff but no money was much less poor than having no money, no big house, and no stuff.

While Elsie sat at the table fretting, Rupert dashed around snapping pictures.

So one day Elsie took him to the soup kitchen where her brother Bob Pocket worked when he wasn't building websites. "Sure," said Bob as he ladled out large steaming bowls of stew, "I'd be happy to build Rupert a website."

"I'm going to be his business manager," Elsie announced.

While they were having this conversation, Rupert looked around. He liked it here. There were all sorts of people: young and old, fat and thin, pretty and ugly, surly and friendly, smelly and clean, speaking all different languages. He had brought his camera, and all these new faces were making his fingers twitch with excitement. "You have to ask permission if you want to take pictures," Bob Pocket told him. "Each person?" whispered Rupert, turning pink.

The soup kitchen.

Elsie, overhearing, rapped on the stew pot with the ladle. Everyone stopped chewing and looked at her. She pointed to Rupert with the ladle. "Stand up, Rupert," she ordered. Turning even pinker, Rupert obeyed.

"This little boy is Rupert," said Elsie. "He's not much for words, but he's a dab-hand with a camera, and he would take very nice pictures of all of you. Raise your hand if you object."

Rupert kept his eyes down and waited for the laughter he was sure would follow. But no one laughed, and no one raised his or her hand – not one person. They settled back on their benches and began to eat again.

"That's settled then," said Elsie. "Have at it, Rupert."

"This little boy is Rupert," said Elsie.

Rupert turned on his camera and snapped away, from every possible angle. The only time people laughed was when he got his head stuck trying to take a picture of legs through the rungs of a chair. He would have hung from a chandelier and snapped, if there had been a chandelier.

Bob Pocket built Rupert a website with a shopping cart and hooked it up to paypal, and Rupert filled it with pictures from the soup kitchen. Within a very short period, his work had gained an online following. The shopping carts began to fill, and money began to trickle in. They only had to sell the worst of the knick-knacks and jewels to make ends meet.

"Say 'soup!'" Rupert thought (but he never would have said it.).

Since Elsie had decided to be Rupert's business manager, Rupert decided to be her assistant gardener, and the arrangement worked nicely. In their spare time they went to help out in the soup kitchen.

Rupert helped Elsie in the garden. The arrangement worked out nicely.

And every now and then, something happened to Elsie's face that might almost have been called a smile.

The end...

...but the beginning of a whole new life!

Rupert & Elsie:
Return to the Pookatina Kingdom

For Sophie and Rebecca

The day had been a busy one for Rupert and Elsie. Rupert was planning an exhibition of his photographs and had been at the gallery all day, measuring the walls. Elsie had worked in the garden all morning and had helped her uncle Bob at the soup kitchen in the afternoon. They were too tired to cook and so had just poached 2 eggs for their supper and had them on toast.

While Rupert did the washing up, Elsie sat at the kitchen table reading the newspaper and commenting on the news to Rupert. Rupert hummed to himself and between his humming and the running water couldn't hear a word she said.

On page five, a tiny little article, illustrated with a blurry photograph, caught Elsie's eye. The half-inch title said, "Rumors of Coup in Pookatina Kingdom".

"Look at this, Rupert," Elsie said.

Rupert stopped humming and came to look over her shoulder. "Pookatina Kingdom..." he read.

"...is my old home," Elsie finished. Elsie's last name had been Pookatina before it was shortened to Pocket, and she had been none other than Her Royal Highness, the Princess Elsina Pookatina.

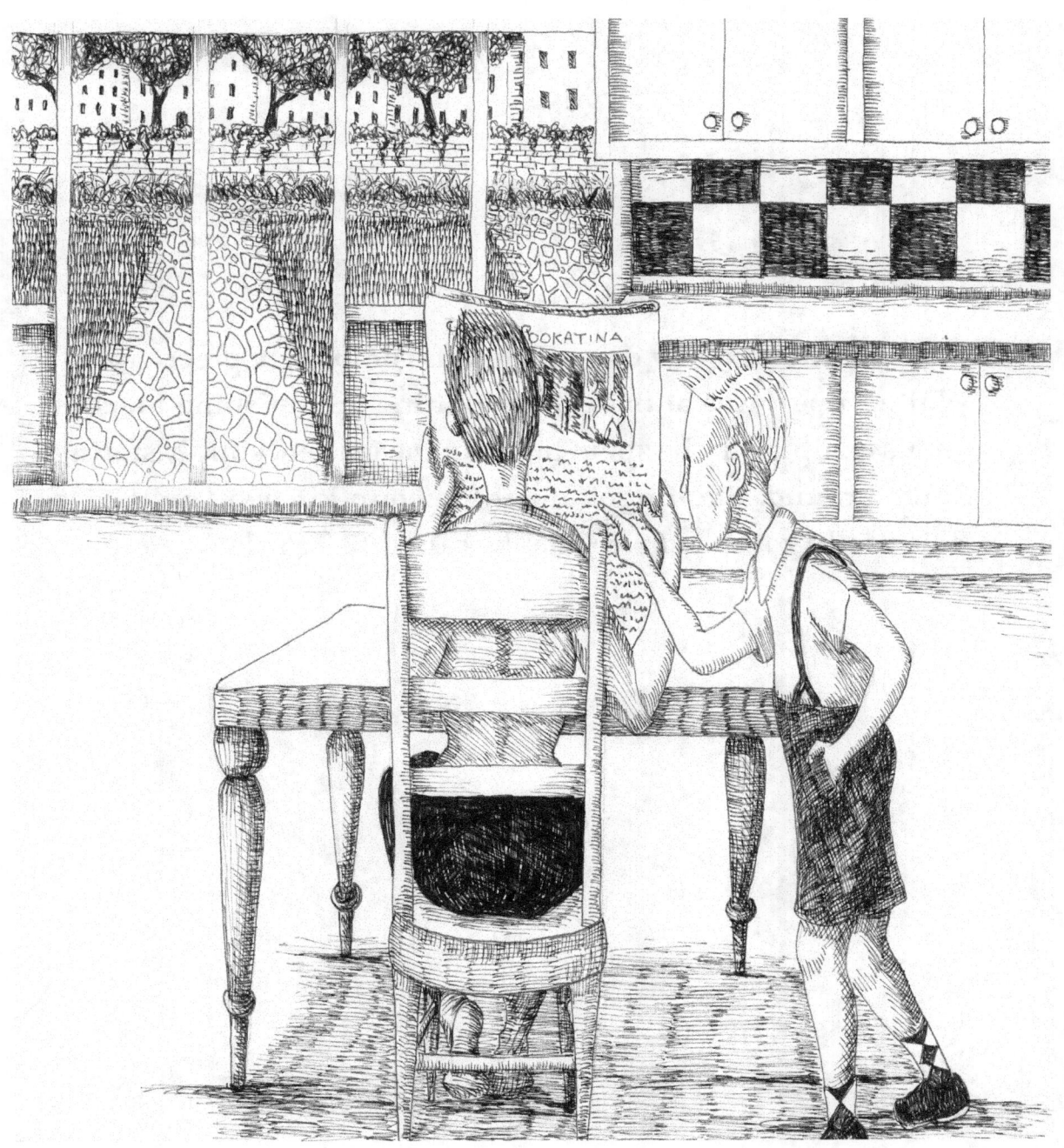

For the next few days, Elsie was completely preoccupied. While Rupert was at the gallery putting the finishing touches on his exhibition, she spent hours in the garden, simply staring at the ground. She forgot about the soup kitchen, and Uncle Bob finally got so worried that he called 13 Truffle Avenue.

Rupert had just come in from the gallery and answered the phone. "Hi, Rupert," said Bob. "Is Elsie okay? She hasn't been to the soup kitchen in days."

"I'm not sure," said Rupert slowly. "She's standing in the garden staring into space. Apparently, there's been a coup in the Pookatina Kingdom. But don't worry, Bob, I'll look after Elsie."

"I know you will," said Bob. "In the meantime, I'll see if I can find out exactly what's going on out there." Bob had been the favorite younger brother of Elsie's father, Lord Oliver, but the royal life never suited him so he had left the Pookatina Kingdom long ago, as a very young man.

But try as he could, Bob couldn't find out anything. After those few sentences and that fuzzy photo in the *Times* – a total Pookatina news blackout

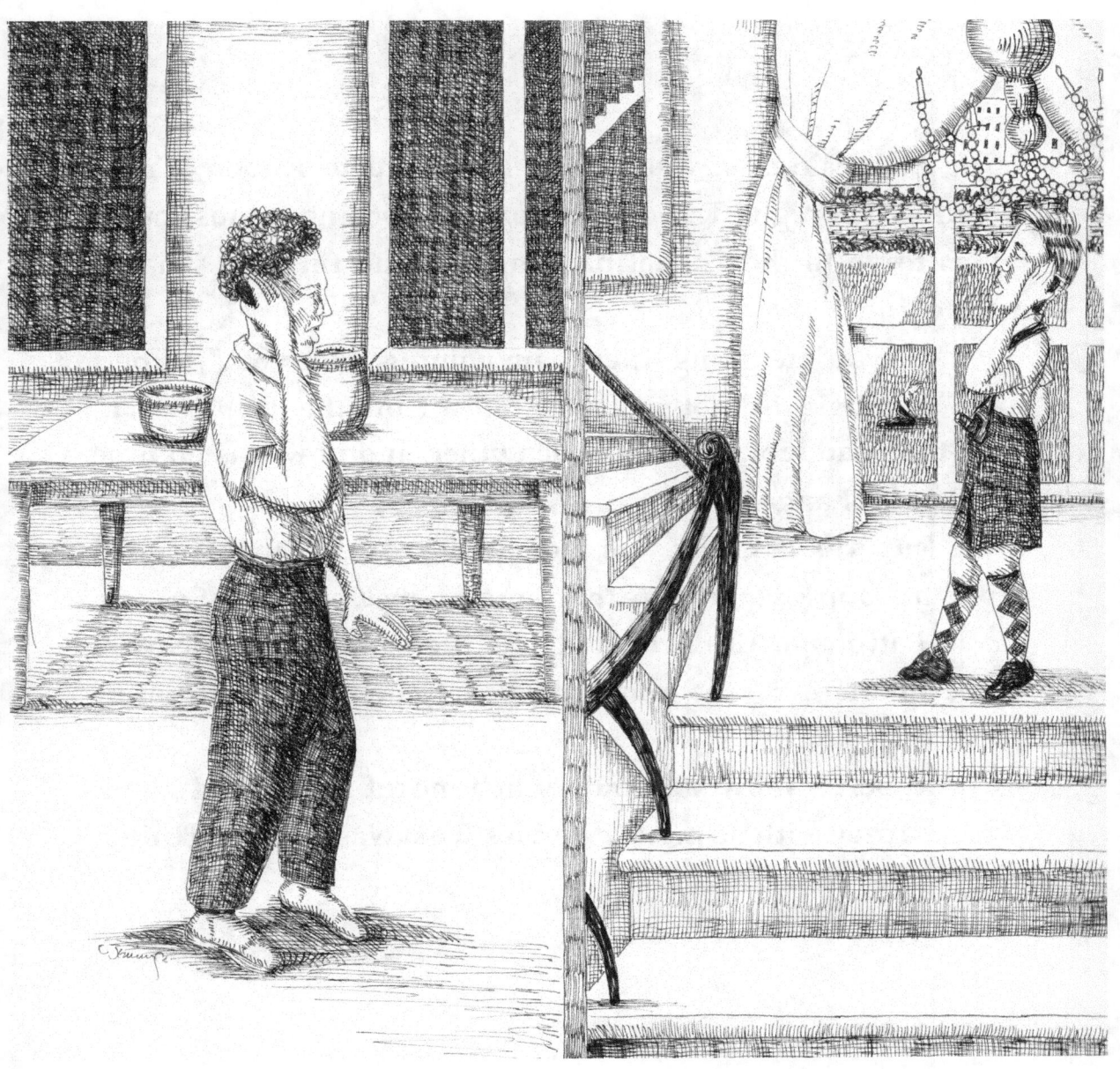

At breakfast a week later, Elsie said to Rupert, "Your opening is tonight, Rupert. Tomorrow morning, I must make plans to go to the Pookatina Kingdom and find out what is happening."

"If you are going, then I am coming with you," Rupert said, and Elsie did not protest. Almost from the day they had met, they had looked out for each other, and now was no time for that to change.

Rupert's opening was a great success. All their friends from the soup kitchen were there, including Uncle Bob. So were many Patrons of the Arts, and The Press, snapping pictures. Rupert thought it was ironic for them to be taking pictures of pictures.

Rupert's show sold out, which meant they could go on their journey with no money worries. That was a very big thing.

The next day, Elsie went to see the travel agent, who responded to her request for two air tickets to the Pookatina Kingdom with a stare of total ignorance. Like most people, she had never heard of the place. Elsie tried to explain where it was, but the woman obviously had a geography-deficiency, and her eyes glazed over as she spoke.

Finally Elsie gave up and bought two tickets to Paris, France. She thought that she and Rupert could make their own way from Paris to the Pookatina Kingdom. Besides, that way they had all the time in the world to actually *see* the world. She smiled as she paid for the tickets.

A week later, Elsie and Rupert arrived in Paris.

Although their own home town was very beautiful, Paris was like nowhere else, especially to Rupert, who had never traveled much at all. They exhausted themselves with three days of sight-seeing and then spent two whole days eating and people-watching in the Luxembourg Gardens. but at the end of it, they had to get going, for they had a destination to get to. In their enjoyment of Paris, they hadn't forgotten that mysterious little article with its fuzzy little photograph.

They took the night train to Venice in a sleeping car, which they shared with two nuns and a traveling salesman. The traveling salesman drank a half-bottle of wine and ate a baguette with fromage (which is cheese in French) and went right to sleep, but the nuns stayed up playing cards in their wimples and nightgowns, and taught Elsie and Rupert to play Bridge and Crazy Eights. After several rousing games they finally slept, and awoke when the train pulled into Venice.

They stepped into a water taxi, which took them to the island of Guidecca, where they were staying. Casa Frollo was actually an old palazzo that had once been very grand, but its owner, Signore Giancarlo, had fallen upon hard times and took paying guests so he could make ends meet.

Oddly enough, one of the guests, whom Rupert discovered in the overgrown garden hidden behind the house, was reading a book titled *Histories and Mysteries of the Pookatina Kingdom.*

"My goodness!" Rupert exclaimed involuntarily.

The girl (for it was a girl) looked up, slightly annoyed at having her peace disturbed. "Qua?" she said, in a peeved tone, which changed when she laid eyes on Rupert, who was exactly her age.

He pointed to her book. "That's where we're going," he said.

The girl laughed. "Good luck. The Pookatina Kingdom is obviously make-believe." Rupert didn't want to argue with her, so he said a polite good bye and went to find Elsie.

Elsie meanwhile had been searching for a boat to take them across the sea. Eventually she found herself at the cruise ship terminal, wandering among the huge floating party cities and feeling a little despondent.

"Could I be of service?" asked a burly person with oiled black hair. "My name is Lavinia."

"Rupert and I need to go to the Pookatina Kingdom." Elsie said.

Lavinia looked concerned. "I was there once, back in the days of Lord Oliver. It was nice then, but the current ruler, Lord Frederick, is a very wicked man. Still, if you need to go, I will take you across the sea in my little boat, but after that you will have to make your own way."

The next day, Lavinia took them across the sea, down the Adriatic into the Mediterranean, through the Suez Canal into the Red Sea, and finally, to the city of Aqaba. The journey took many days and they made no stops. Rupert sat in the back of the boat and waved whenever Lavinia would shout out the name of the land they were passing. "That's Greece! Now we're in Egypt!" And when they arrived in the port of Aqaba, she said, "This is as far as I go. I have to get home for my cousin's wedding. Anyway, it's all inland from here." Which Elsie, of course, already knew.

It was hard-going from there. Aqaba was surrounded by sea, mountains, and desert, and while everyone had heard of the Pookatina Kingdom, no one had ever actually been there or knew exactly where it lay. It had gained a legendary status over the ages, a Nabataean kingdom in the midst of modernity, and if it weren't for the fact that Elsie herself was living proof of its existence, most people would just assume it was a fairy tale.

They purchased a camel and loaded her with food, water, blankets, a change of clothes for each of them, and gallons of sun block. It was so hot in Aqaba that Rupert wondered why they needed blankets. "The desert gets very cold at a moment's notice, especially after sundown. Now slather on your sun block, Rupert – lots of it. You have very fair skin and don't want a sunburn."

It was a long and arduous journey. They had no guide, since no one really knew the way; all they had were an ancient map and Elsie's memories from the time when she and her mother had made their escape, many years earlier.

They traveled up the steep and rocky mountains and across the parched desert. They lost track of time. But just as they were running out of food, Elsie began to recognize the terrain. They had begun the steep climb into the mountains surrounding the Pookatina Kingdom.

It took them a whole day to climb to the summit, where they could look down onto the kingdom below, with its sweeping desert plains, its oases and the glinting turrets and minarets of the city. From a distance, it all looked the same - and just as beautiful - as Elsie remembered it.

The next day, as they made their way toward the city, they were confronted by warriors holding swords and spears.

"Who are you?" asked the leader of the warriors. She was a wiry, tough woman old enough to be Elsie's mother, or Rupert's grandmother.

Elsie tried to explain. "I am Elsina Pookatina," she said, "Lord Oliver's daughter." And to Rupert, she seemed to grow a little taller and a great deal more haughty.

The warriors didn't believe her and began to move forward, weapons aloft, when their leader held up her hand. "Wait," she said. "Of course you are Elsina – I can tell by your springy short hair. You never could wear a tiara - it always bounced off."

All the warriors bowed, except the old woman, who hugged Elsie tightly. "Welcome home!" she cried. "We thought you were dead. I am your Auntie Ansook. Do you remember me?"

Elsie smiled happily, but the truth was she barely remembered Auntie Ansook, who as a younger person had always been off hiking in the mountains with her boyfriends.

Elsie introduced Rupert. Auntie Ansook told Rupert and Elsie everything that had happened in the years since Elsie fled: how Uncle Frederick had fooled everyone for the first few months, until food began to run short, and his selfishness began to be known.

"But the last straw was when everyone learned that he had nearly killed Lord Oliver before imprisoning him and that Lady Zaha and Princess Elsina had fled for their lives."

"*Almost* killed?" said Elsie. "I thought my father was dead."

"Oh no," said Auntie Ansook. "Frederick may be a very bad man, but even he is not really a vicious killer."

"And my father?" asked Elsie.

"Your father is fine, but weak, after years of prison. And he's old too, Princess. Don't be too shocked when you see him. He will be overjoyed to see you, and to know that you have come back to rule, now that he is old."

Now the truth was, Elsie had no desire to rule the Pookatina Kingdom, or even to live there. She had grown used to the modern world, just like Uncle Bob, and she loved her nice home with Rupert at 13 Truffle Avenue.

When they entered the city, the streets were lined with citizens. Word of their Princess Elsina's return had already spread, and they welcomed her with loud cheers and big hugs. They welcomed Rupert too, even though they didn't really know who he was.

"The first thing we must do," said Elsie, " is get Uncle Frederick out of that palace, so that everyone knows he has no power anymore."

So they marched to the palace, with Elsie at their head, and she used an old key that had always been on her keychain to unlock the door in the garden wall. She held up her hand for everyone to wait for her outside the wall. Except for Rupert. "Come on, Rupert," she said.

The two crept quietly through the garden, which had once been very beautiful. No one had taken good care of it in quite awhile, and the sad plants were badly in need of a good drenching.

"We'll do that next," said Elsie, reading Rupert's mind. "But first, Uncle Frederick..."

At last they found him, smelly and unkempt and much older even than his years, sitting in the throne room talking to a group of cockroaches. But even the cockroaches no longer paid him much heed.

"Uncle Frederick!" Elsie said sternly.

A faint glimmer of recognition appeared in the pathetic old man's eyes. "Elsina?" he said in a quavering voice. And burst into tears.

"He needs a bath," said Rupert. They got him into the bathtub, so that he would be more presentable before anyone else saw him. He wasn't a good man, but Rupert and Elsie felt sorry for him. Once he was clean, they took him to a little house on the palace grounds, where he lived out his days as happily as a bad old man could, cared for by a nurse who was so cheerful that he drove Uncle Frederick crazy, just as he deserved.

Once Uncle Frederick had been sorted, Elsie went to see her father. He was lying in bed at Auntie Ansook's house and just as Auntie Ansook had warned, he was very, very frail. But the moment he laid eyes on Elsie he looked ten years younger!

"I thought I'd never see you again!" he said, holding her hand very tightly in both of his.

"And I thought you were dead!" replied Elsie.

"Wonders never cease," said Rupert, his eyes filling with happy tears as he watched the wonderful reunion. Although it must be said, his tears were - a little - for himself, since he was pretty sure Elsie would be staying in the Pookatina Kingdom as its ruler and he would have to return alone to the big old house at 13 Truffle Avenue.

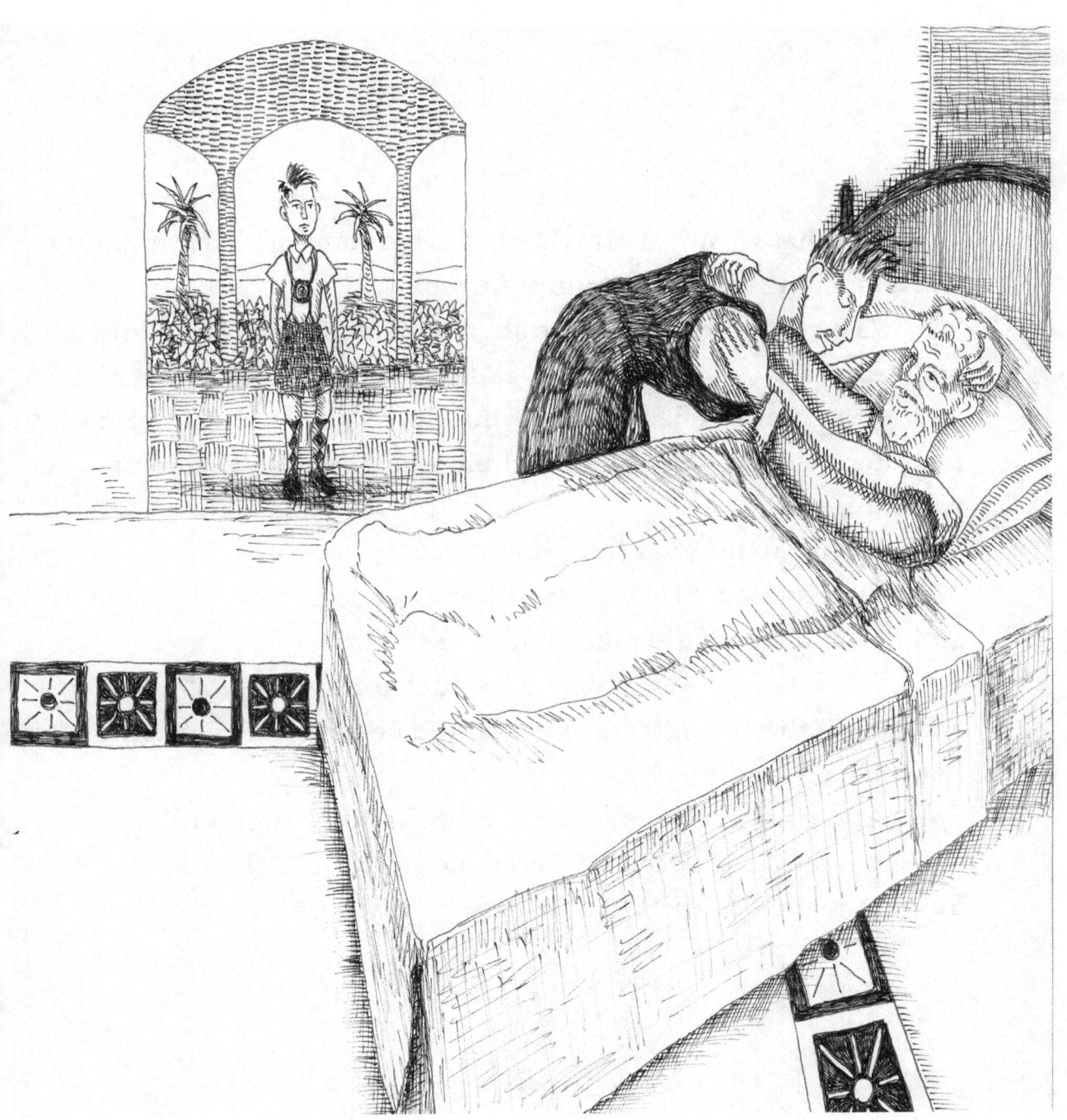

But that wasn't at all what Elsie had in mind. That night she had a long talk with Auntie Ansook.

"You don't really want to stay in the Pookatina Kingdom and be its Lady, do you Elsina?" asked Auntie Ansook astutely.

"No," said Elsie. "I think you know what's best for our people now, and you have children who could help you and rule after you."

"What about your father?"

Elsie smiled. "He would like to come to live with Rupert and me, and we would take good care of him."

"I know you will, my dear," said Auntie Ansook. "If you and your father are agreed, then I would be honored to lead the Pookatina Kingdom."

And so, after a month in the Pookatina Kingdom Elsie, Rupert, and Lord Oliver headed home to Truffle Avenue. Before they left, Rupert took a royal family portrait.

The journey home was even more fun than the journey to the Pookatina Kingdom had been. Auntie Ansook had made sure that they traveled in style, and Lord Oliver looked younger by the day. He couldn't believe his eyes, as he got to see the wide world beyond the Pookatina Mountains. He and Rupert and Elsie laughed the whole way home, and Rupert had thousands of great photo opps for his next exhibition.

When they arrived home, the garden was in full bloom, and Uncle Bob -- who was, after all, Lord Oliver's baby brother -- had taken care of everything. He had even prepared a wonderful feast of spaghetti and meatballs, so they all sat down to eat.

"I like adventures very much," said shy little Rupert, looking happily at his adopted family from his place at the head of the table. "But I like being home even better."

The End.

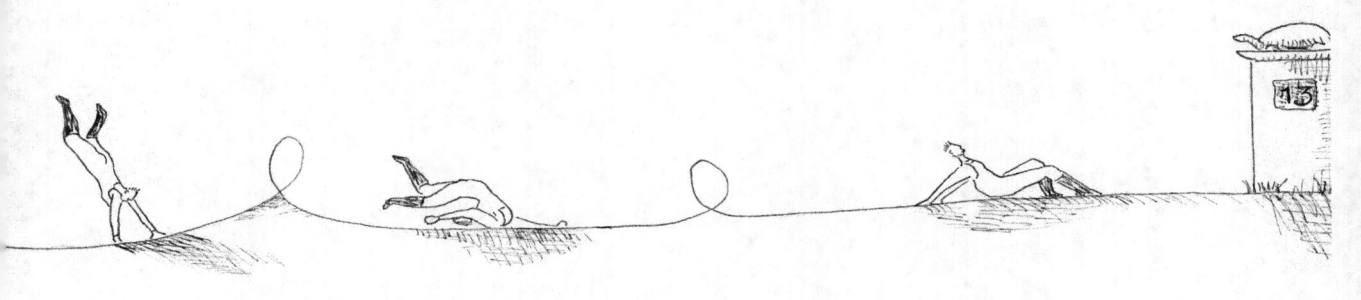